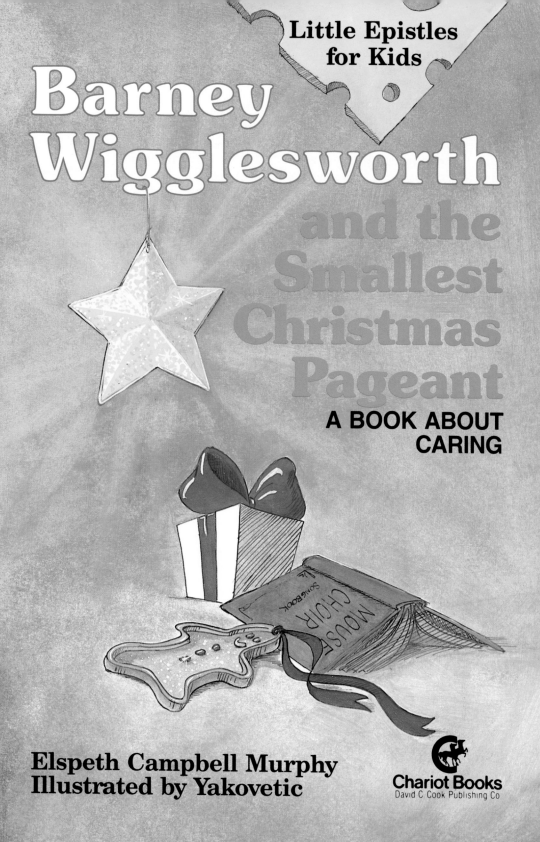

Little Epistles
for Kids

Barney Wigglesworth and the Smallest Christmas Pageant

A BOOK ABOUT CARING

Elspeth Campbell Murphy
Illustrated by Yakovetic

Chariot Books
David C Cook Publishing Co

Rejoice with those who rejoice; mourn with those who mourn.
(Romans 12:15, NIV)

Dear Parents and Teachers,

Barney Wigglesworth and the Smallest Christmas Pageant is a story illustration of Paul's exhortation to the Romans.

The words are so simple, even catchy, that we might think they're easy to *do*. Not so. It's hard enough for us as adults to put ourselves in another's place and share someone else's feelings. It's even harder for little kids!

Children are all bound up in how they feel—both physically and emotionally. It's asking a lot for them to set that preoccupation to one side and think how the world looks from another person's point of view. Such empathy doesn't happen overnight, but growing in understanding and compassion for others is an important part of friendship and Christian maturity.

This story takes place at Christmas when the mice, like us, are more preoccupied than ever and inclined to assume that everyone's feeling joyful. But Gwendolyn Scoot has met with difficulties, and she needs her friends to imagine themselves in her place and come to her aid.

But why mice? It has been said that animal characters are really "kids in fur coats." Children will readily identify with Barney, Gwendolyn, Tillie, and Sam. But because animal characters are one step removed from real life, the concepts of the book come across in a fun, nonlecturing, nonthreatening way.

So join your kids in crying and laughing along with Barney and his friends!

Chariot Books is an imprint of David C. Cook Publishing Co.
David C. Cook Publishing Co., Elgin, Illinois 60120; David C. Cook Publishing Co., Weston, Ontario
BARNEY WIGGLESWORTH AND THE SMALLEST CHRISTMAS PAGEANT

Cover design by Dawn Lauck
First Printing, 1988   Printed in Singapore
93 92 91 90 89 88 5 4 3 2 1
Library of Congress Cataloging-in-Publication Data
Murphy, Elspeth Campbell.
  Barney Wigglesworth and the smallest Christmas pageant. (Little epistles for kids)
  Summary: Barney and his mouse friends cheer up and help Gwendolyn, the Christmas pageant director, during a crisis.
  [1. Caring—Fiction. 2. Mice—Fiction. 3. Christmas—Fiction. 4. Christian life—Fiction]
I. Yakovetic, Joe, ill. II. Title. III. Series.
PZ7.M95316Baw   [E]   88-5009
ISBN 1-55513-686-9

It was Christmastime again, and I (Barney Wigglesworth) was in charge of decorating the tree in the church sanctuary. So I had to go around to the other church mice kids to collect the decorations they had made.

I found Gwendolyn Scoot on the set of the Christmas pageant, where she was directing four little actors.

"Lovely entrance, darlings!" she said to them. "Simply lovely! But we need a little more—how shall I put it?—*emotion*. This is your big scene, so let's give it all we've got, hmmm?"

Then she turned and saw me as I was picking up her pile of decorations. "Barney! How absolutely marvelous of you to drop in on our little rehearsal!"

(Did I mention that Gwen is the dramatic type?)

"Are you sure I can't interest you in being in the pageant?" she asked.

"No, thanks!" I said. "I just came for the decorations."

"Ah, well . . ." said Gwendolyn with a sigh. She turned back to her actors. "Darlings! Please don't sneeze and shiver like that! It's not in the script. Now, once more—with *feeling*!"

My next stop was Tillie Nibbles. Tillie's mouse hole opens off the church kitchen. Her whole family was busy making the most delicious Christmas cookies for the party after the pageant. Tillie was having a wonderful time. But she couldn't stop to talk, so I just got her decorations and went on to Sam Scurry's house.

Sam's mouse hole opens into the choir room. It gets pretty noisy over there when rehearsals are going on. I guess that's why Sam always talks so loud. Anyway, Sam wasn't home. Mrs. Scurry told me he and his five older brothers were out Christmas caroling. So I just got Sam's decorations and hurried back to the tree.

There is *nothing* more fun than decorating a
Christmas tree. I felt wonderfully happy.

On my way back home I passed Gwendolyn.

Right away I could tell something was wrong. "Gwendolyn, what's the matter?" I asked.

"The pageant is ruined, and I am devastated," she said.

"Why, what happened?" I asked.

"My actors all came down with the most absolutely devastating colds," cried Gwendolyn. "And I have no one to replace them. Oh, what am I going to do?"

"Cheer up, Gwennie," I said. "It's not the end of the world!"

"Oh, what do you know?" sobbed Gwendolyn. "You just don't understand!"

"I don't understand what's wrong with Gwendolyn,"
I said to Tillie and Sam. "How can anyone be sad when
it's Christmastime and the tree is all decorated?"

"And the cookies are all baked," said Tillie.

"AND THE CAROLS ARE ALL SUNG," said Sam.

Tillie frowned thoughtfully and said, "Of course, Gwen was really looking forward to the pageant. I *feel* for her. I can imagine how terrible it would be if—say—my oven broke down, and I couldn't bake cookies."

"You're right!" I said. "I feel for her, too. Imagine how terrible it would be if my Christmas tree fell over!"

"YOU'RE RIGHT!" said Sam. "I FEEL FOR HER, TOO. IMAGINE HOW TERRIBLE IT WOULD BE IF I LOST MY VOICE!"

We decided to help Gwendolyn out. We hurried over
to her mouse hole in the Sunday school supply closet.
"We'll be in your pageant," we said. "Just tell us
what to do, and we'll do it."

Gwendolyn could hardly believe her ears. "Oh, this is absolutely the most wonderful thing that ever happened to me!" she said. "Now let's hurry and get into our costumes."

"Costumes!" I said. "Now wait just a minute. I didn't know anything about this. I feel for you and all that, but I am *not* going to be in the Christmas pageant wearing some silly costume!"

It turned out that the pageant was a huge success.
At the party afterwards, Gwendolyn was the
happiest of all.

"You are such good friends," she said to Tillie, Sam, and me. "When I was sad, you were sad along with me. And now I'm happy, and you're happy along with me."

Late that night, after the party, we tiptoed back into the sanctuary and whispered to one another, "Merry Christmas!"

THE END